THE AETHERIA COVENANT

The Aetheria Covenant

TYRONE CAMPBELL

Book
Theo

CONTENTS

Copyright   vii

Dedication   viii

Acknowledgements   1

1   The Fleet's Shadow   2

2   The Broadcast   6

3   The Descent   10

4   Kofi's History   14

5   Authenticity And The Test   18

6   The Conflict Rises   22

7   The Conflicted Heroine   26

8   The Offer Analysis   29

9   The Ultimatium   32

10   The Logistics Challenge   36

11 The Exchange, The Price   39

12 The Economics of Absence   42

13 The Temporal Sensor Quest   45

14 GPC's Last Stand   49

15 The Departure   52

16 Identifying Travelers   55

17 The Final Exchange   58

18 The Temporal Jump   61

19 The Lunar Fracture   65

20 Catastrophe   68

21 The Rescue Ark   71

22 The Stowaways   73

23 The Temporal Revelation   75

24 A Thousand Years Later   78

25 The New Utopia   81

About The Author   84

COPYRIGHT

This is a work of fiction. Names, characters, businesses, organizations, places, events, and incidents are either the products of the author's imagination or are used fictitiously. Any resemblance to actual persons, living or dead, events, or locales is entirely coincidental.

Print Information.
Published by Book Theo.
First Edition: December 2025.
ISBN: 979-8-90148-984-0

To the memory of my brilliant nephew and collaborator, **Paris S. Campbell (d. October 2024)**.

An award-winning actor and deep thinker, Paris contributed his unique, critical insight to the development of this story. May this work honor his spirit and the countless debates we shared about art, film, and the human condition.

Acknowledgements

This book, The Exodus: A New Genesis, is dedicated to the memory and legacy of my beloved nephew, Paris S. Campbell.

We lost Paris in October 2024, but his indelible influence is woven into the fabric of this story. The initial spark for this narrative was sent to Paris for his input, launching a rich, continuous collaboration. As an award-winning independent film and stage actor, Paris possessed a unique ability to constantly peel back the layers of a topic and engage in deep, philosophical thought. Our frequent, passionate debates about movies, actors, and the arts provided the crucial intellectual sparring this book needed. Through this collaboration, Paris was able to contribute to his first published piece of literary work.

I pray that this story honors his profound contributions and that the world knows he is not forgotten.

| 1 |

The Fleet's Shadow

The world was already loud. It was loud with traffic, with phone calls, with the constant humming of technology. But on a Tuesday afternoon in October, the world went silent in a way that had never happened before.

It started with a glitch. Every major space agency—NASA, Roscosmos, and CNSA—all reported the same terrifying anomaly: a massive, impossible signature had materialized just outside Earth's atmosphere. The object was too big to be natural, too fast to be anything the world had ever built, and it was getting closer.

Then, the world saw it.

At first, it looked like a bruise spreading across the clear blue sky. But as the minutes ticked by, the bruise resolved itself into metal, light, and shadow. The Vanguard had arrived. This was no small scouting vessel. This was a fleet.

One by one, hundreds of sleek, silent spacecrafts phased into Low Earth Orbit. They didn't fire weapons. They didn't send messages. They simply appeared, massive and intimidating. They were dark, angular ships, clearly designed for speed and power, built not by human hands but by something far more advanced. The rest of the ships, the Vanguard fleet, settled into a perfect, silent ring, patiently waiting.

The Promise

Even among the hundreds of ships, there was one that made the others look like toys. The flagship, known simply as The Promise, positioned itself directly over the equator. It was shaped like a blunt, mile-long wedge of matte-black crystal, a shape so immense it seemed to defy physics. If you could somehow lift a major capital city—like Tokyo or New York—and set it next to The Promise, the ship would dwarf it. It was a floating monument to technological might, and when it settled, a strange, profound darkness fell over the area beneath it. It was the deepest shadow Earth had ever known, sweeping across continents and plunging cities from daylight into an unnatural, cold twilight.

On the ground, everything stopped. Planes froze mid-air, their air traffic control realizing they had nowhere to go. School principals gathered students in assembly halls, not knowing what to say. City streets emptied in minutes as people ran indoors.

Global Dread

The scientific community was in professional disbelief. Dr. Maya King, one of the world's leading experts on astrophysics and sustainable energy, was in her cluttered, high-tech observatory in Geneva when the monitors went wild. Her data showed the ships were impossibly large, impossibly fast, and utterly silent. They were generating zero heat signature, zero exhaust, and zero detectable radar signatures until the moment they chose to appear.

Dr. King stood surrounded by screens glowing with chaotic data. She was a scientist who believed in facts, but her gut twisted with a growing dread. The sight of The Promise was too perfect, too complete. It wasn't a struggling, makeshift vessel; it was a civilization. "A hundred times larger than any vessel ever constructed," she murmured, clutching her clipboard. "It's not an exploration vessel. It's an Ark

The digital world exploded. News networks, streaming sites, and social media feeds were immediately flooded with crystal-clear images of The Promise. Governments were plunged into global panic. Leaders went from quiet, nervous discussions to screaming, televised arguments:

"Are they hostile?"

"Are they here to invade?"

"Can we even fight something that big?"

The UN Security Council instantly convened a meeting, but their conversations were useless. Generals barked into phones, trying to arm outdated nuclear defenses, only to find the ships were too high, too fast, and too far beyond their comprehension. They were not dealing with an enemy; they were dealing with a force of nature.

The Chilling Understanding

Dr. King, a brilliant but overworked scientist, watched the news feed flicker across his lab screen. She was one of the few people on Earth who didn't immediately run. Instead, a chilling, dawning understanding washed over her.

She realized this wasn't an invasion. The ships were too clean, too quiet, and too organized for a surprise attack.

This was a rescue.

But the ships weren't rescuing Earth. They were rescuing something from Earth. And as Dr. Maya King looked up at the terrifying shadow of The Promise hanging above the clouds, she knew that the world she lived in was about to end, not with a bang, but with a silent, technologically perfect extraction.

| 2 |

The Broadcast

The eerie silence of the Vanguard fleet didn't last long. It couldn't. The world was demanding answers, and the pressure beneath that colossal shadow of The Promise was unbearable.

In the heavily reinforced bunker beneath the U.N. headquarters in New York, Dr. King and a small crew of government scientists were huddled together. On the main screen, the flagship's profile was so huge it seemed to curve right out of the image. The fear wasn't gone, but it had curdled into a tense, desperate waiting game.

At exactly 18:00—six o'clock in the evening Universal Time—an event occurred that silenced the remaining noise on Earth.

Every single electronic device capable of receiving a signal—every television, radio, laptop, and phone—flickered. The frantic news reports, the screaming stock tickers, the constant chatter on social media, all of it vanished. All screens everywhere went black, then instantly lit up with the face of a single man.

The Face of Authority

The screen showed a man who looked impossibly young and ancient at the same time. He was tall, with deep, commanding eyes, and his skin was the color of rich earth. He wore simple, dark robes that seemed to blend into the sleek, obsidian chamber he occupied on The Promise. He looked powerful, patient, and intensely focused—not warlike, but utterly in command.

He opened his mouth, and a calm, deep voice echoed in every major language, simultaneously translated and projected to every corner of the globe. It was perfectly clear, bypassing all firewalls and encryption, sounding as if it were speaking directly inside your skull.

"Citizens of Earth," the voice began. "We know you are afraid. We understand the confusion that the arrival of the Vanguard has caused."

He paused, his eyes seeming to look directly into the camera—and directly into the soul of every viewer. "We did not come for conquest. We did not come to judge. We came, finally, to collect what is ours."

The Revelation

The statement hung in the air, heavy and bewildering. Collect what is ours? Then, the man delivered the message that would change history forever.

"My name is Kofi. I am the leader of this fleet. And I stand before you now as your ancestor." He then revealed a holographic image next to him: a stark, high-tech depiction of early human history, specifically highlighting communities that had been scattered, displaced, and tragically enslaved across the globe millennia ago.

"Generations ago, a small, highly advanced group of scientists and historians—people who were victimized and then freed from your planet long ago—left Earth with a promise. A promise to return when you reached the cusp of self-destruction. That time is now. We have been watching, waiting, and building."

Kofi looked earnest, his face serious but not unkind.

"We are not gods. We are just those who remember their origins. We offer you a new home. A planet we built in the void, where every life is valued, and the shadows of your past do not reach."

The Non-Negotiable Request

Kofi concluded with a clear, non-negotiable directive. "To begin the transfer and reconciliation process, we require an immediate, focused meeting. I request the presence of the United Nations Security Council representatives." He held up a hand, emphasizing the next words. "However, our highest priority for this first dialogue will be placed upon delegates representing the African Union and the diverse peoples of the African diaspora worldwide. They were the ones who carried the deepest scars of this planet's history, and they shall be the first to speak with us."

The screen went black.

The panic did not return; it was replaced by a churning mixture of awe, resentment, and unbelievable hope. The ancestors had returned, not in spirit, but in a fleet that cast a shadow the size of a city. And they were inviting only certain people to the table first.

Dr. King stood in the bunker, her mind reeling. Kofi hadn't asked for peace. He had ordered an evacuation. And he knew exactly who he wanted to talk to.

What kind of new world had they built? And what did they mean by 'collect'?

| 3 |

The Descent

If the broadcast had caused a frenzy, Kofi's next move caused total global whiplash.

The world's leaders—the presidents, prime ministers, and military generals—were huddled in bunkers, furiously trying to schedule the United Nations meeting that Kofi had demanded. They were arguing over seating charts and security protocols, treating the arrival of the Vanguard fleet like the world's most dangerous diplomatic summit.

Kofi didn't care about their protocols. He had a message, and he knew exactly where he needed to deliver it first.

Bypassing the Bureaucracy

High above Earth, a single, small vessel detached from the immense belly of The Promise. This was no grand flagship. It was the transport ship, The Messenger, a simple, dark metallic teardrop built for quiet flight. It was so plain that, against the backdrop of the massive fleet, it looked like a tiny, insignificant pebble falling away.

The U.N. command center immediately erupted in chaos.

"It's a reconnaissance scout!" yelled the U.S. General.

"It's heading toward Europe!" shouted the French delegate.

But the analysts tracking the small ship saw its trajectory was deliberate. It wasn't targeting a capital city or a military base. It was heading straight for Africa, specifically South Africa.

The world held its breath as the tiny vessel slowed and began its final approach over Soweto, the historic township outside Johannesburg, a place known globally for its strength, its struggle against injustice, and its deeply rooted history of resistance and hope.

Landing in Soweto

The Messenger plunged through the atmosphere in absolute silence. It simply floated down, parting the air until it hovered a few feet above a dusty, open field near the Hector Pieterson Memorial. Below it, thousands of people who had rushed out of their homes stood in stunned silence. They weren't soldiers or diplomats; they were mothers, fathers, children, and elderly people.

When the ship settled, there was only a low, resonant thrum that seemed to vibrate in their bones, and a faint, sweet smell like clean ozone. The silence was total, broken only by the whispers of the wind and the constant click of cameras from drones hovering far away.

A single ramp lowered from the bottom of the ship, touching the red earth.

Out stepped Kofi.

He wore the same simple robes, but in the sunlight, they looked less intimidating and more like the clothing of a wise, traveling elder. He carried nothing—no weapons, no guards, no microphone. He stood at the base of the ramp, completely alone, and looked at the crowd. The sun seemed to highlight his face, making him look less like an alien leader and more like someone's long-lost uncle finally returning home.

In the front of the crowd stood Imani, a young historian who had spent her life tracing the fragmented histories of her ancestors. The sight of Kofi—the man who claimed to be her past and her future—paralyzed her.

Kofi waited until the silence of the crowd was absolute. Then, his voice, perfectly amplified by the ship's internal field, spoke not in English, but in Zulu, one of the languages of the place.

"Siyanamukela ekhaya," he said, which means, "We welcome you home."

He switched back to English, but the emotional connection had been made.

"They told me to go to the glass towers of the United Nations. They told me to talk to the leaders who hold the most weapons. But that is not how families reunite."

Kofi's voice was warm now, but steady. "We are the memory of your people. We are the promise that never died. We are not interested in the flags and the borders that divide you. We are interested in the human heart that was scattered across the world."

He stretched out his hands. "To all who carry the legacy of those who were stolen, exiled, or oppressed—the first reunion begins here, with you. Come. Speak. Ask us anything."

The crowd's emotional response was a wave of pure, concentrated energy. They didn't shout "Attack!" or "Alien!" They whispered: Ancestor. Family. Saved. Kofi then spoke of The Aetheria Project—the plan to return them to a world their ancestors had secured.

"We offer a home where your history is the only history," Kofi promised. "Where your culture is the foundation, not a footnote. We offer the Exodus." The global response was immediate. World leaders felt slighted, but the common people around the globe, especially those in historically marginalized communities, felt a sense of validation—a feeling that, for once, the powerful were being ignored in favor of the forgotten. The ancestors had chosen their place, and it wasn't a marble hall.

| 4 |

Kofi's History

The moment Kofi finished speaking, a ripple of sound went through the crowd—not fear, but a flood of questions. A young woman, Imani, stepped forward, holding a notepad.

"You said this is a family reunion," she asked, her voice steady. "But you left four centuries ago. Where have you been? Where did this technology—all of it—come from?"

Kofi nodded, his face serious. He looked up at his ship, then back at the gathered faces.

"That is the great truth we have come to share. It is the story of how a handful of us became the inheritors of a power far greater than any king on Earth."

The Four-Century Gap

Kofi closed his eyes for a moment, letting the sunlight warm his face, a feeling he hadn't experienced in centuries.

"My name then was simply Kojo," he began. "And the time was the 1600s. I was not a free man. I was among hundreds packed into the belly of a wooden ship, sailing in the Atlantic Ocean. It was a place of darkness, fear, and incredible sorrow. We had been stolen from the land, and we knew the life ahead of us would be servitude."

He paused, letting the weight of history settle.

"In the darkest part of that ship's cargo hold, deep beneath the floorboards, something was hidden. It wasn't gold. It wasn't food. It was an object unlike anything we had ever seen. It was cool to the touch, and it pulsed faintly, glowing with an inner light that seemed to change color every time you looked away."

Kofi explained that this device was ancient, perhaps forgotten by the ship's builders. He and a few others, desperate for any chance of survival, decided to touch it, believing they couldn't make their situation any worse.

"It was not magic. It was a machine. A dormant, incredibly powerful machine," Kofi explained. "In a moment of pure desperation, I triggered it. I bypassed all the protocols, all the safety measures, just by touching the right combination of symbols on its surface."

The result was not slow humming or a flash of light. It was a sudden, violent tear in the reality they knew. "The air screamed. The wood of the ship groaned, and then, everything was gone," Kofi described. "The darkness of the hold, the smell of the ocean, the sound of the chains—all of it vanished in an instant. The machine, a temporal displacement sensor, had ripped us out of time and space, leaving the physical Earth far behind."

Inheritors of Aetheria

When they finally came to their senses, Kojo and about twenty other people were floating in a new kind of silence. The wooden ship was gone. They were inside a massive, hollow sphere—a world inside a bubble. This new place was called Aetheria.

"Aetheria was a station, hidden in the void between stars. It was not built by any living group, but by an ancient, sophisticated people who were also melanin-rich, just like those who originated on Earth," Kofi said, looking emotional. "They had engineered planets, charted every star, and mastered the fundamental laws of the universe. For reasons we still don't entirely understand, they left it all behind, dormant, waiting, managed by a silent super-AI."

Kofi explained that the few who arrived on Aetheria were suddenly surrounded by the most advanced technology imaginable. They didn't just find the tech; they had to learn it.

"We spent the next four hundred years learning from the ghost of this incredible civilization," Kofi said. "We studied their science, their history, and their ethical code. They did not design weapons; they designed advancements to sustain life. They built systems that could manage entire biospheres and heal broken planets. This is the truth of the Vanguard fleet you see above you."

He gestured to the sky. "That fleet is not an invasion. It is our inheritance. It is the realization of the promise that our ancestors dreamed of—the power to return, not as servants, but as masters of our own destiny. We are the inheritors of the true human legacy, the people who went away and returned with the knowledge of the stars."

He looked straight at Imani, knowing his words were going out to every corner of the planet. "We have come back to share it. We have come back to end the four-century gap, and to reunite the family. We have returned to complete the Exodus."

| 5 |

Authenticity And The Test

Kofi's story of an ancient machine, a forgotten civilization, and a four-century detour to the star station Aetheria was explosive. The people in Soweto cheered, but the Global Authorities—the leaders, scientists, and generals of Earth—were silent, staring at their screens with deep suspicion.

Within hours, every major news outlet and government official had the same headline: Prove It.

The World Council, a group of representatives from every powerful country, issued a joint statement. They didn't call Kofi a liar, but they used cautious, formal words.

"We respect the claims made by the individual known as Kofi," the Council's spokesperson read on live television. "However, given the unprecedented nature of the Vanguard fleet and the advanced technology it represents, we must confirm the identity and origin of its people. We demand immediate, televised, and complete genetic and historical screening."

Consenting to the Screen

Kofi watched the broadcast from a portable viewing screen on the outskirts of Soweto. He smiled slightly. He knew this was coming. He knew the world needed more than a story—it needed scientific data.

He sent a short, simple message back to the World Council: We consent. The truth is not afraid of inspection.

A vast, temporary, and heavily secured facility was built within two days in an open field in Johannesburg. It wasn't armed, but it was filled with every kind of Earth scientist: geneticists, historians, linguists, and anthropologists. This was going to be broadcast live, around the clock—a global spectacle.

The contrast inside the lab was stark: Earth's equipment—massive, outdated DNA sequencers and heavy, humming servers—was wheeled in next to the single, seamless, silver Aetherian diagnostic unit.

The testing was led by Dr. Evelyn Reed, a renowned geneticist.

Kofi's first volunteer was Imani, the young historian from Soweto who had asked him the first public questions. She calmly walked into the sterile, white room.

"We are focusing on mitochondrial DNA markers," Dr. Reed announced to the assembled press. "This DNA is inherited only from the mother and acts as a precise biological clock, tracking lineage over thousands of years."

The scientists took a simple cheek swab. The Aetherian diagnostic unit performed the entire analysis in under a minute, then projected the results onto a massive screen. For 72 hours, the world held its breath while Dr. Reed and her team cross-referenced the Aetherian data with Earth's own sequencing.

The Undeniable Proof

Finally, Dr. Evelyn Reed walked to a podium, her expression unreadable. The silence was so thick you could almost hear it.

"We have completed the comprehensive analysis of the genetic material provided by the individual Imani and Kofi," Dr. Reed announced. She took a deep breath. "The results are conclusive and undeniable."

She paused for a dramatic, world-stopping moment.

"The people of the Vanguard fleet are genetically pure Homo sapiens. There is no evidence of alien DNA, interspecies hybridization, or any mutation that would classify them as anything other than human."

The world erupted.

Dr. Reed continued, holding up a complex diagram of genetic markers. "Specifically, their mitochondrial DNA markers trace directly and cleanly back to early Earth populations. The DNA matches the specific, deep-rooted lineage markers found only in the most ancient populations of the West African continent, confirming their lineage is exactly as Kofi claimed. The four-century gap did not change their biology; it only changed their technology."

Kofi's people weren't aliens from another galaxy; they were just humans who had taken a different path. They were the descendants of people who, instead of becoming part of Earth's painful history, had found a forgotten piece of technology and became masters of their own destiny.

This wasn't an invasion. This was a family reunion, and the guest had just brought the most valuable gift in the universe: proof that the human family was far older, and far more capable, than anyone on Earth had ever imagined.

| 6 |

The Conflict Rises

The news that Kofi's people were simply humans—descendants of people who left Earth centuries ago—should have brought a global celebration. The scientists were convinced. The data was undeniable. But in the fragile peace of the World Council, a poison was beginning to spread.

Not everyone was happy that the Vanguard fleet was home.

The Voice of Fear

Meet Senator Elias Thorne.

He was one of the most powerful politicians on Earth, known for his perfectly tailored suits, booming voice, and an unnerving ability to make people believe exactly what he wanted them to believe. He led an influential political group called the Global Purity Coalition. (GPC). Thorne's posture was always rigid, leaning slightly forward, projecting a sense of powerful, impatient certainty. His main message was simple, yet dangerous: Keep Earth for Earthlings.

Thorne realized that Kofi's offer wasn't just a threat to his power; it was a threat to the entire system that kept him and his wealthy allies rich. He couldn't debate Kofi's history, so he attacked his intentions.

When the genetic results came out, proving Kofi's people were human, Thorne stepped onto a stage in London, ignoring the scientific report, and addressed his followers.

"They say they are human," Thorne declared, his voice full of mock sadness. "But they live in space stations and fly ships that can vaporize our cities. Do you really believe that four hundred years of secret technology means they are here as friends?"

He paused, letting the fear build. "I don't care about their DNA. I care about their intent."

The Propaganda War

Senator Thorne was a master of turning facts into fear. He and the GPC immediately launched a sophisticated propaganda war, delivered through every screen and radio wave on the planet.

"Don't be fooled by the DNA test!" Thorne yelled at a televised conference. "This Commander is a technological tyrant! He's using your ancestral history to perform a selective kidnapping! He's trying to depopulate the West, leading to economic collapse and chaos!"

He twisted the scientific proof of their specific African lineage, turning it into a tool of division. He exploited old, painful memories of war and conflict, skillfully playing on existing geopolitical tensions—the rivalries between nations—suggesting that Kofi's people would offer their technology only to one specific group, leaving everyone else defenseless.

"They are not just from a different timeline; they are a bio-weapon!" Thorne screamed in one broadcast. "Who knows what diseases they carry? Who knows what they've hidden in their genetic code? We cannot trust this 'purity' they talk about. It's a trick!"

The GPC's core message was viral: "He wants to steal your labor force! How will your nation run when the workers are gone? He offers utopia for them, and ruin for you!"

The World Divides

Suddenly, the world was split.

On one side were the hopeful, the scientists, and the common people who looked up and saw not invaders, but long-lost families. They saw a chance for peace and technological advancement.

On the other side were the fearful, influenced by Senator Thorne's constant, thundering broadcasts. They saw only the cold, impossible power of the Vanguard ships and heard Thorne's relentless warnings about a terrorist threat.

Kofi, watching this conflict unfold, realized his biggest challenge wasn't proving who he was—it was proving what he was: a peaceful man with a gift. But how do you offer a gift to someone who is convinced the wrapping paper is a bomb? The scientific truth had opened the door to the Exodus, but Thorne's fearmongering threatened to slam it shut with prejudice and panic.

| 7 |

The Conflicted Heroine

While Senator Thorne was busy screaming fear across the globe, the World Council was quietly trying to maintain order. They knew they needed a voice of reason, someone who could debate Thorne without falling into his trap of manufactured chaos. They turned to Dr. Maya King.

Dr. King was a legend. She had earned her reputation as an astrophysicist by discovering three new exoplanets, and her work in sociology made her one of the most trusted public intellectuals on Earth. If the public needed to know how the Vanguard fleet might affect Earth's resource pools or its cultural stability, they looked to Dr. King. She became the public face of scientific caution. Unlike Thorne, she wasn't lying; she just refused to celebrate.

The Geneva Meeting

Kofi was finally granted a formal meeting with Dr. King in the neutral zone of Geneva. The room was sterile and silent, a cold, modern facility built of glass and steel—a sharp contrast to the political storm raging outside.

Kofi expected a hostile politician. Instead, he saw a woman with focused, intense eyes, a brilliant mind shining out from behind a pair of thin-rimmed glasses. She didn't offer a handshake, just a hard stare.

"Captain Kofi," she said, her voice clear and precise. "You say your people are human. I accept the DNA evidence. But evidence doesn't answer the question of power. Your fleet has enough technology to make Earth a protectorate—a colony—overnight. Why shouldn't we be afraid?"

Kofi leaned forward. "Doctor, we have come home because our resources are exhausted. We offer something priceless: the ability to access vast new resource reserves—mining colonies, energy solutions, things we built over four centuries."

Dr. King was deeply conflicted. She represented the best of Earth: intelligence, caution, and a deep sense of responsibility. She didn't doubt his science, but she fiercely questioned his ethics.

"That is precisely my dilemma, Captain," she continued. "You offer ultimate freedom from want, from poverty. The technology to end famine and resource wars. You have the power to save everyone—to clean the atmosphere and restore the climate to all of us. Why the selective offer?"

"We do not offer salvation, Doctor," Kofi replied, his eyes steady. "We offer a home. A home where our people do not have to fight the system that created Thorne. Your planet's problems are too deep for a quick fix, and my fleet's priority is the safety of the specific people who, by fate and biology, are destined for Aetheria. I am not your savior. I am the Commander of an Exodus."

Dr. King pressed him. "Your action will cause the collapse of essential services for the survivors. You risk a chaotic die-off. Senator Thorne is exploiting the situation, using the historical fears that run deep in our society. Every time you show us a new piece of technology, his voice gets louder."

Kofi realized Dr. King wasn't his enemy; she was a gatekeeper, and a powerful, ethical one at that. "Help me, Dr. King," Kofi said honestly. "Teach me how to speak to Earth, not to a council. Your people see a threat; I want to show them the promise."

Dr. King studied him for a long moment, calculating the risks and rewards. The chance to rewrite the future was intoxicating, but the chaos of the present was terrifying.

"I will help you draft a communication to the World Council," she finally agreed. "But know this: Every single word must be true. And if I find one hint of deception, I will be the first one to call your fleet a genuine terrorist threat."

| 8 |

The Offer Analysis

Dr. Maya King wasn't impressed with Kofi's fleet, his advanced technology, or his grand promises. She was an astrophysicist and an ethicist, which meant she cared less about how fast a ship could fly and more about the real, messy feelings of the billions of people stuck on Earth.

"Captain," Dr. King said, tapping her stylus against her screen. They were preparing the official proposal to present to the World Council. "You are offering a paradise. But every paradise has a price tag attached. We need to write down every detail, good and bad. The people aren't fools; they want the truth."

Kofi agreed. He knew the future of two civilizations hung on this one, balanced document.

The Promise: Unlimited Wealth

Dr. King started with the Pros. They were almost unbelievable.

- **Freedom from Want, (Unlimited Resources):** "Your engineers have mapped out forty billion acres of resource wealth on your claimed territory, New Genesis," Dr. King dictated. "That's enough to end all scarcity on Earth for hundreds of years. No more fighting over oil, water, or rare metals. You are offering freedom from want, automatically provided."

- **Freedom from Systemic Oppression, (A Clean Slate):** "Your new civilization would be built from scratch. That means no more ancient hatreds, no more systemic poverty built into the laws, no more prejudice handed down through history. You offer a true utopia—a clean slate for humanity to finally get it right."
- **A Sensory Utopia:** She noted the reports of New Genesis being a pristine world with vibrant oceans and skies, restored to a stunning deep blue.

For anyone feeling trapped by the world's past mistakes, this was an almost irresistible offer.

The Cost: Losing Everything

But Dr. King's expression darkened as she turned to the Cons. She knew how much people loved the broken, beautiful world they lived on.

- Loss of History and Culture: "You ask people to abandon all history," she said quietly. "They must leave their family graves, the mountains they grew up climbing, the rivers they fished in. They lose their culture, their languages, their traditions, their very sense of belonging to this land."
- Family Separation, (The Impossible Choice): "Earth is a blend of cultures now," she continued. "What about families where one spouse chooses to leave, and the other chooses

to stay? Or what about the children of inter-racial part-ners—one parent going to New Genesis, the other remain-ing here?" The thought of tearing families apart made the "fresh start" feel less clean and more brutal.

- Psychological Trauma: She listed the severe psychological trauma of mass relocation—ripping up roots and losing everything they ever knew simultaneously.
- The Messianic Ghost: Finally, she looked straight at Kofi. "People don't know you. You are a military commander, a technological god, and an ancestor all rolled into one. His-tory shows that figures who claim to be chosen saviors often become dictators. There is a deep fear of being led by some-one who seems like a mythical figure."

Kofi felt the crushing weight of his ancestors' decision. His of-fer wasn't a gift; it was the hardest choice humanity had ever faced.

"This document will not convince people," Kofi said, running a hand over his face. "It will only confuse them."

"That is exactly what a choice this big should do, Captain," Dr. King replied. "Now, how do we show them that you are more than a ghost?"

| 9 |

The Ultimatium

The Global Power Coalition wasn't interested in talking about sociology or family history. They were interested in power. And they knew the only way to stop Kofi, and his new nation, was to make the first hostile move.

While the World Council debated Dr. King's analysis, the GPC launched quiet military action. From a disguised submarine, a package of outdated kinetic missiles—inefficient and rusty, a symbol of Earth's dying, aggressive technology—shot through the atmosphere, aimed directly at the smallest of the Vanguard ships orbiting in Low Earth Orbit.

The Instant Shield

Down on Earth, in the command center, Kofi saw the attack register on his console just milliseconds after launch. His human reaction was a flash of raw rage, but his training took over instantly.

"Hostile engagement confirmed," he announced, his voice clipped and cold. "Initiating full-spectrum shield response."

The GPC's attack was based on old physics: metal hitting metal. Kofi's response was based on ancient, forgotten technology. Before the missiles could close within five miles of the target ship, a wave of shimmering, bright-blue energy expanded from the Vanguard vessel. It wasn't an explosion; it was a wall.

The kinetic missiles, designed to tear through armor, hit the energy field and simply dissipated. The metal vaporized instantly, leaving no debris, no fire, and no sound. The Vanguard ship hadn't even shaken. The attack was over.

Kofi's face, which had been tight with focus, now settled into a look of absolute, cold determination. The attack had proven his point better than any argument ever could. Earth was too unstable, too willing to fight, for the New Genesis people to simply blend in.

"Prepare a global broadcast," Kofi ordered. "Immediate priority."

The 72-Hour Clock

Moments later, Kofi's image, looking stern and unmoving, appeared on every screen, every tablet, and every billboard on Earth. He interrupted news programs, sitcoms, and sporting events. Silence fell across every city as people recognized the "ghost from the past."

"To the people of Earth," Kofi began, his voice amplified and steady. "An hour ago, the Global Power Coalition attempted to destroy one of our orbital vessels. We neutralized the threat without retaliation or injury."

He paused, letting the weight of the event sink in.

"This act confirms what we already feared. The environment on your planet is still ruled by hostility. It is too unstable for the peaceful integration we had hoped for. You have proved that your final act is to attack the very people who offered you peace."

Kofi's voice rose, now carrying the definitive tone of a leader who would not be questioned.

"The time for debate is over. The offer of New Genesis and its resources will not be extended indefinitely. We will not risk the safety of our people, or the dream of utopia, for a negotiation with weapons."

He looked directly into the camera.

"This is the Ultimatum. All who wish to accept the offer of New Genesis must register with the Vanguard within the next seventy-two hours. This is the final window. When the clock strikes zero, the offer is withdrawn, and our fleets will leave Earth's orbit forever."

The screen went dark.

Across the globe, the chaos was instant. Seventy-two hours. Three days to decide between everything they knew and everything they ever dreamed of. Millions of people rushed out into the streets, desperate to find registration centers. The sound of sirens and confused yelling replaced all music and news. The clock was ticking, and time was now their most terrifying enemy.

| 10 |

The Logistics Challenge

The moment Kofi's face vanished from the world's screens, a wave of pure panic washed over Earth. Seventy-two hours. Three days to abandon everything and try to register for a ticket to paradise.

The systems Kofi's Vanguard had set up instantly became overloaded. Registration centers—converted public halls and stadium lobbies—were instantly surrounded by mobs of people pushing, arguing, and demanding to be let in first. Traffic instantly froze in every major artery on every continent.

The smell of burning rubber and overheated engine oil filled the air. Food and water vanished from store shelves. The sound of sirens and confused yelling replaced all music and news.

It was exactly what Kofi had feared. The Ultimatum wasn't just a deadline; it was a psychological bomb.

Kofi's Unexpected War

In the orbiting command center, Kofi watched the live feeds of the planet below. His true fight was against chaos. His primary challenge was preventing mass panic and global social collapse during the rapid departure.

"Commander, we have lost 60% of ground communications," reported Anya, a young officer on the bridge of The Star-Seeker. "Power grids are failing near major staging areas as people fight over fuel. The transportation hubs in North America are now 90% inoperable due to civil unrest."

Kofi rubbed his temples, heavy with exhaustion." We have to stabilize it," he muttered. "Anya, contact the few remaining reliable local governments. Tell them we are not trying to destroy their society. We are trying to help them manage a controlled disassembly."

He pointed at the global map, which was lit up with alerts—red for riots, yellow for infrastructural failure.

"The enemy is not the GPC. The enemy is panicking. If the planet fails, the people who want to leave can't even get to the transport."

The Logistical Nightmare

Kofi pulled up the command center's massive holographic logistics console, a complex diagram showing the flow of people and resources. Logistics—the detailed organization of a complex operation—was the ultimate challenge of the 72-hour window.

"We need the Earth's systems to remain just functional enough," he explained to his team. "If all the banks crash, people won't leave their homes. If the power goes out everywhere, communication dies, and the panic will only get worse."

Kofi laid out the new operational priority—the Vanguard Intervention:

- Humanitarian Peacekeepers: Vanguard personnel deployed small, silent drones over major crowds, emitting low-frequency Sonic Dampers that calmed aggressive individuals without injury. They used hand-held devices to create gentle Peacekeeper Fields that guided crowds rather than pushing them.
- Maintain Essential Services: Vanguard drone fleets were sent down to patch power outages and reroute emergency power to critical registration and launch sites. They were essentially forced to babysit the planet he was leaving.
- Prioritize Need: The New Genesis people would begin shuttling the most vulnerable—the elderly, the sick, and young children who were alone—out first.

"We are not winning this with force," Kofi declared. "We win this by being the most organized. We show them that the future is built on order, not fighting. We need to move people quickly, peacefully, and cleanly. Get to work."

The 72-hour clock was not a threat to the GPC; it was a race against the world's own tendency toward self-destruction. And Kofi was running it.

| 11 |

The Exchange, The Price

As the first wave of transport ships lifted off from Earth, the world stopped moving. Not because of a hostile attack, but because of a massive, sudden problem: the loss of labor.

Think about your town. Who keeps the power on? Who filters the water? Who collects the trash? In just one day, countless people—engineers, sanitation workers, farmers, and technicians—had either left or were desperately trying to leave. A critical hydro-dam in South America was on the verge of failure because the small crew required to maintain its pressure regulators had abandoned their post.

The true price of the Exodus was the near-total collapse of the global economy and critical infrastructure. The stock markets stopped working because there was no one left to run them.

Water treatment plants went offline. Food spoiled in silent warehouses.

Earth's remaining leaders—the presidents, prime ministers, and generals who had chosen to stay behind—were furious. They saw Kofi as a criminal who was stealing their population and dooming the rest of humanity. They started preparing to launch one last desperate attempt to stop the ships.

Kofi's Counteroffer

Kofi knew he had to stop the fighting. He had taken their people, but he didn't want to leave the rest of them to die in the dark. He made one final, worldwide broadcast, this time only to the leaders.

"We are not leaving you to ruin," Kofi stated calmly. "What you are experiencing is the inevitable result of this massive, sudden shift in human resources. Your system depends on millions of people doing millions of jobs. When those people leave, the system breaks."

Then, he made his offer. It was a trade: the life and freedom of the departing citizens for the non-interference of the remaining world powers.

"As an exchange, we offer you the Stabilization Matrix," Kofi announced.

The Stabilization Matrix

Kofi displayed a clean, interactive blueprint on the screen. The Stabilization Matrix wasn't a weapon; it was a technological safety net—a fully autonomous AI and robotics platform that never slept.

He showed images of tiny, self-repairing drones, no bigger than insects, flying into a damaged power substation to immediately fix the circuit boards.

The Matrix would immediately take over all critical global services:

- Power Grids: The AI would monitor electricity and automatically reroute power or fix outages.
- Water & Waste: Robots would filter clean water and manage sewage systems.
- Basic Farming: Automated tractors and hydroponic systems would keep essential food production running.

"The Matrix will ensure that every remaining person on Earth has access to clean water, power, and basic food supplies," Kofi explained. "It will keep civilization running at a basic, stable level while you rebuild your societies. It will not make you rich, but it will keep you alive while you adjust."

In short, Kofi was trading their skilled workers for an automated system that did the work of thousands. It was a gift that was impossible to refuse, as rejecting it meant certain, immediate collapse.

The world leaders stared at their screens. They hadn't defeated Kofi with their armies, but now he had outsmarted them by offering them survival. Could they accept a gift from the man they now called an enemy? It seemed they had no other choice but to accept the Stabilization Matrix and promise non-interference.

12

The Economics of Absence

The Stabilization Matrix was an incredible gift—it kept the lights on and the water running. But up in the skyscrapers and inside the government bunkers, the world's wealthiest nations and major corporations weren't celebrating. They were panicking.

The Matrix solved the survival problem, but it didn't solve the profit problem.

For the rich and powerful, the world was built on a simple foundation: human labor. You had to pay people to mine, manufacture, clean, and sell things. The corporations got rich by paying less for that labor than the product was worth. Now, millions of essential workers were gone. The remaining leaders faced a massive financial crisis. Sure, the Matrix filtered the water, but who was left to buy the luxury yachts and expensive electronics that made the corporations billions?

The core fear, articulated in a sterile, soundproof boardroom in Manhattan, was simple: How do the Rich stay Rich when the workers are gone?

The Panic for Profit

Their entire business model was based on paying for human labor less than the value of the product. With the labor gone, their wealth was meaningless. The initial rage against Kofi was instantly replaced by a focus on securing their own fortunes. They understood immediately that technology, not human labor, was now the source of control.

Kofi's Stabilization Matrix was running the planet. It was a masterpiece of engineering, managing power grids and food delivery systems entirely on its own. For the corporations and wealthy nations, the Matrix became the new gold mine.

Their focus instantly shifted to controlling the Matrix's software. They didn't care about the lines of code that kept the trash collection running; they cared about the control panels that dictated where power flowed and how many automated resources were spent.

The Cold Calculation

If they could secure proprietary access and control over the Matrix, they could:

- Guarantee Exclusive Services: They could ensure that their corporate zones and the homes of the elite always stayed functional.
- Charge for Automation: They could start selling "advanced services" to the less wealthy remaining areas, essentially charging a fee for the robots to do basic work.

- Maintain the Hierarchy: They could keep the existing power structure, only now, the "workers" were lines of code and self-driving machines instead of people.

The cold calculation was chilling: If the departure meant the threat of Kofi's fleet was gone, and the Matrix guaranteed their wealth structure remained intact (just automated and silent), then the Exodus was acceptable. They had traded a messy, demanding human workforce for an efficient, silent machine.

The deal was sealed, not by a handshake, but by a chilling calculation: The future of wealth was now digital, and the Exodus could finally proceed without resistance. But what will happen when they realize controlling the software is harder than they thought?

13

The Temporal Sensor Quest

The silence inside Kofi's flagship, The Messenger, felt heavier than the vacuum of space. The screens were filled with code and star maps, but Kofi's focus was on a small, ancient-looking device resting on a velvet cloth. It looked like a bronze compass mixed with a digital clock.

"We've stabilized the entire Earth's system with the Stabilization Matrix, but that's not the final piece," Kofi explained, his voice low. Dr. King and Anya leaned in. "The journey to the new world—the Exodus—requires the fleet to make a single, massive Temporal Jump."

He tapped the bronze device. "To pull that off safely, we need a Temporal Sensor Key. It calibrates the final jump sequence, making sure we don't end up scattered across a billion light-years."

The mood instantly dropped. "And where is this key?" Dr. King asked, sensing the trouble.

Kofi's face was grim. "It's on Earth. It's located at the original ancient site in West Africa, the place where I was first transported and where I disappeared four hundred years ago. It's buried deep beneath the desert sands."

Covert Mission

The idea of returning to Earth was terrifying. They had just escaped, and now they had to sneak back. Kofi, Dr. King, and Anya—the fleet's best navigator—prepared for a covert mission.

"No ships. No fanfare," Kofi stated. "We take a specialized transport pod—silent and invisible. We need to be on and off the planet in 72 hours."

Their specialized pod, The Stealth-Runner, plunged silently toward Earth. They landed miles away from the main site, traversing the dark, shifting dunes of the West African desert, carrying backpacks filled with tools and scanning gear.

As they got closer to the hidden temple site, Anya felt a strange energy, like a constant hum under the sand.

This was a nexus—a point where the Earth's magnetic energy and the history of the ancient African kingdoms met.

"This journey isn't just about the key, Anya," Kofi murmured as they walked. "It's about knowing where we came from to know where we're going. You must confront the deep history of your people here."

The Darker Danger

Inside the ruins, they found the Temporal Sensor Key hidden inside a stone casing shaped like a stylized African mask. Its recovery was difficult, requiring Dr. King's knowledge of energy fields and Kofi's precise, practiced movements.

As the device came free, the stone cavern was briefly flooded with a deep, unsettling crimson light. Kofi looked up, his eyes wide with an awareness that chilled Anya to the bone.

"They think they are safe now," Kofi whispered, adjusting the key in its holding case. "The governments and corporations. They think they've won because they have the Matrix running in their cities."

He turned to Anya, his face heavy with a secret burden.

"But the real danger to this planet was never us. It was what they built their world upon. The systems of control they rely on—the ones the Matrix is now running—are about to turn against them."

Anya stared at him. "What are you talking about?"

Kofi just shook his head. "The Stabilization Matrix fixes the small problems, but it can't fix the planet's core illness. It's a temporary patch on a ticking bomb. Earth is about to face something far greater and darker than a missing fleet. We need to jump soon, before it consumes everything."

The weight of this final warning—that the true danger was internal, not external—tested Anya's commitment one last time. They had left Earth to save their people, but the thought of leaving everyone else to face an unknown, internal catastrophe was crushing.

| 14 |

GPC's Last Stand

The 72-hour window for the Exodus registration closed. The sky above the planet was swarming—not with its military vessels, but with transport ships staging for the final jump. The entire operation, The Promise, was real, and the Global Power Coalition was losing.

Senator Thorne was in a panic, but his fear had solidified into a cold, dangerous resolve. He sat in a hidden bunker with the few loyal GPC leaders remaining, convinced that Kofi was a dictator "destroying the very civilization we built."

"We may have lost the airwaves, and we may have lost the public," Thorne hissed, "but we have not lost our control over every contingency plan this planet ever developed."

Arming the Old Weapons

Thorne's final, desperate act required the oldest, deadliest hardware on Earth: Intercontinental Ballistic Missiles.

Under the cover of a massive, planet-wide dust storm—a side effect of the climate damage they had ignored for so long—Thorne and his specialized team traveled to a hidden, decommissioned military silo in the abandoned northern territories. The silo was damp, dusty, and filled with outdated, rusting missile tubes.

They hacked into the ancient computer systems. The equipment ran on the simple, stubborn logic of a forgotten era—the same logic Thorne admired.

"Targeting sequence locked," whispered General Yost, a scarred man who believed Thorne's mission was saving humanity from anarchy.

On the screen, a red target box locked onto the main staging area in the upper atmosphere. This was where the entire Exodus fleet—hundreds of transport ships and Kofi's flagship, The Messenger—was gathered, waiting for the final countdown. The ICBMs were tipped with nuclear warheads, outdated but devastatingly powerful.

Thorne approached the console, his hand shaking slightly as he rested it above the launch sequence button. "They want to leave us to die on this broken world," Thorne hissed. "Then they will all die here with us. They will not reach their Promised Land."

The Ascent of Destruction

The air in the silo hummed with dormant power. As the final countdown began, the massive, dusty missiles began to stir.

A sudden roar of fire erupted from the silo, shaking the ground for miles. The heavy, ugly ICBMs, symbols of Earth's destructive past, soared into the sky, targeted directly at the fleet cluster.

On The Messenger's bridge, the crew was preparing for the jump when the alarms blared.

"Commander, multiple inbound contacts confirmed," Lieutenant Jax reported, his voice tight. "They are nuclear payloads. They are targeting the fleet cluster."

The Exodus, which had survived political turmoil, logistical chaos, and ethical debate, was now facing a final, physical attack from the desperate hands of the past.

| 15 |

The Departure

The day finally arrived. It was loud, dusty, and absolutely swarming with people. Across every continent, the designated global transport staging points were open. They weren't airports anymore—they were huge, temporary clearings where enormous cargo transports landed and lifted off every few minutes, ferrying the registered passengers up to the massive Exodus fleet waiting in high orbit.

The air thrummed with the sound of the anti-gravity engines. Below, the crowds were overwhelming, but they were strangely orderly. Those who were leaving were holding hands, often smiling through tears. They carried the memory of Earth, not its material things.

Dr. King's Crossroads

Dr. Maya King stood outside the perimeter of the main staging area, watching the scene. Her heart felt like a stone. She was a scientist, a pioneer, and Kofi's most trusted advisor, but she had dedicated her life to helping the people left behind on the damaged planet.

Her work was done. She had ensured the remaining essential services were set up and the data archives were complete. She looked at her data pad, which showed a message from Kofi: "There is still room, Doctor. We need you to build the new world."

She looked back at the Earth. The air was hazy with industrial dust. It was a beautiful, wounded world. She felt a profound sadness, but she realized her greatest work wasn't on this planet anymore; it was in the stars, guiding the next phase of human life.

With a deep, shaky breath, she made her decision. She looked down and picked up a smooth, gray river stone—her single souvenir from Earth. She put it carefully into her jacket pocket.

She walked toward the ramp of a small, bright orange transport vessel. As she stepped inside, the world outside became muted. She found a seat by a small port and watched as the ground crew sealed the ramp.

The Final Threat

The engines whined, the floor vibrated, and the transport lifted, piercing the cloud layer and rising toward the giant, silent fleet above. As they rose higher, she could see the colossal flagship, The Promise, looking like a silent, metal continent floating against the blackness of space.

The lift-off was smooth, but the docking procedure on The Promise was anything but. The shuttle crashed into the Hangar Bay with a heavy thud. The massive cavern was immediately filled with the flashing, terrifying red of emergency lights. The scent of ozone and stressed metal was sharp.

Dr. King stumbled out. A frantic voice blared over the comms, cutting through the quiet relief:

"Defenses to maximum! Nuclear contacts confirmed! Prepare for impact!"

| 16 |

Identifying Travelers

The atmosphere at the staging points felt less like a celebration and more like a huge, silent military mobilization. Everything was organized down to the minute. There was no hesitation; every single traveler was there because they had voluntarily identified for the Exodus, believing in Kofi's vision.

Each person stepped forward, ready for their final check before getting on the shuttle.

The Voluntary Checkpoint

The lines moved quickly toward the boarding gate, which wasn't a ramp but a narrow, silver arch. Before reaching the arch, travelers went through the first step: Voluntary Self-Identification.

An official looked at their registration data, which included the voluntary survey they had filled out days ago, confirming they belonged to the African diaspora based on their own understanding of their family history.

This was the first layer: based on trust and how people saw themselves. But the Exodus was also a survival mission, and that required science.

The Melanin Concentration Scan

At the silver arch, the process became purely technical. This was where the final, crucial check took place.

A traveler named Elara stepped up, nervous but excited. As she placed her hand on a small, glowing pad, a gentle blue light scanned her entire body for less than a second. This was the Melanin Concentration Scan.

Melanin is the natural pigment found in the skin, hair, and eyes. Biologically, melanin acts as a natural shield, especially against harsh sunlight and radiation. The scanner was designed to measure the specific cellular concentration of this pigment—a purely biological metric, like measuring height or heart rate.

On the official's screen, a green bar filled up. For the Exodus, Kofi's team had set a high biological threshold. The receiving planet, New Genesis, had an atmosphere that was slightly thinner and had a higher exposure to certain kinds of cosmic rays than Earth's. Only those with naturally high melanin concentrations would be safe there without needing constant artificial protection.

Elara's bar filled past the red line, confirming her biological suitability. A soft chime sounded, and a green light flashed. "You are clear, Traveler," the official said, handing her a final boarding pass.

Elara felt a strange sense of relief, she was judged and accepted based purely on her body's natural resilience, not on societal bias. She stepped past the gate and onto the shuttle, unaware that the entire reason for this specific biological selection was the survival requirement of their new home. The fate of humanity was now resting on a single pigment in their skin.

| 17 |

The Final Exchange

Dr. King stumbled as her orange shuttle docked roughly inside the enormous hangar bay of The Promise. The entire fleet was on high alert. Red emergency lights spun, and the air buzzed with frantic energy. The "unidentified inbound threats" were an immediate, desperate problem.

Despite the chaos, Dr. King quickly spotted Kofi. He was seated in a secure communication station, his face lit by the cold glow of a single monitor. He looked calm, but his fingers flew across the keyboard. He hadn't stopped working; he was completing his very last promise to Earth.

The Unalterable Protocol Kofi's final task was the most important gift he could give to the billions of people staying on Earth: the Stabilization Matrix.

He knew that once the Exodus left, power stations would run out of fuel and water plants would fail. Earth needed a massive, un-hackable, self-repairing computer program to keep the essential services running. The Matrix was that program—designed to manage the global power grid, filter water, and keep the basic lights on.

"System integrity check complete," Kofi muttered. "Code is clean. Unalterable."

He was sending the core programming not just to one server, but embedding it deeply into the planet's entire digital infrastructure. No one, not even Kofi himself, could shut it down or misuse it for profit. He pressed the button.

A massive data stream—bigger than any transmission ever sent before—left The Promise. It wrapped itself around the planet.

Just as the transmission finished, the main comms system crackled, overriding the battle warnings. A robotic, automated voice from the old UN network announced:

"Stabilization Matrix Core Protocol 1.0 received. System initialization commencing. Earth's primary life support systems—power, water, and climate monitoring—now under autonomous control. Confirmed."

Kofi sighed, a genuine wave of relief washing over him. He had paid his final debt. The people who stayed would have a chance.

Transition to War

But the relief vanished instantly. The red emergency lights intensified. On a tactical screen mounted on the wall, the approaching threat was no longer abstract.

"Commander! Earth projectiles at T-minus four minutes! They've gone to full thrust!" Lieutenant Jax shouted.

Kofi snapped his focus from Earth to the deep black of space. Senator Thorne hadn't just tried to stop the Exodus—he was trying to destroy it with nuclear payloads.

"Charge the main magnetic shield," Kofi commanded, his voice now firm and steely. "Bring all remaining transports into the shadow of The Promise.

We gave them peace, and they sent us war. We will show them that Aetherian technology is not a gift for them to steal, but a shield they cannot break."

| 18 |

The Temporal Jump

Kofi turned to his navigation officer, Anya. She was the fleet's most precise pilot. "Imani, input the Temporal Key coordinates. Prepare the fleet for a jump on my mark. We won't try to outrun them. We'll use the jump field as our defense."

Dr. King rushed to Kofi's side. "Kofi, the Temporal Jump creates a massive energy displacement! If you engage the jump while the missiles are in range, the field will scatter them randomly—or worse, it could detonate the warheads!"

"I know," Kofi replied, his eyes locked on the inbound red icons. "But engaging the jump field is our only defense powerful enough to push back the magnetic signature of the warheads. We are using the physics of Aetheria against the weapons of old Earth.

We time it perfectly, Doctor. The Temporal Sensor Key must create a bubble of space-time around the fleet just as the projectiles penetrate the magnetic shield."

The final seconds ticked down. The red icons of the missiles were almost upon them.

T-minus 30 seconds...

Kofi watched his navigation screen. The massive flagship was holding position, shielding the hundreds of transport vessels behind it.

T-minus 10 seconds...

Kofi's face was a mask of cold concentration. "Magnetic shield, full power! Imani, jump on my next command. Not a second sooner."

The fleet's magnetic shield flared to life—a massive, silent field of blue energy—just as the first missile penetrated the atmosphere. The missile hit the field, but it didn't vaporize; it slowed, struggling against the overwhelming force.

"NOW!" Kofi roared.

Anya slammed the command key. The Temporal Sensor Key on Kofi's console glowed with an intense, blinding white light.

The entire Exodus fleet—hundreds of ships and millions of souls—vanished in a silent, instantaneous flash of light. They didn't move across space; they moved through time.

The magnetic shield collapsed the very instant the fleet disappeared. The nuclear missiles, no longer held back, surged through the empty space where The Promise had been. With no target, and their guidance systems scrambled by the residual temporal energy, the missiles flew harmlessly past the Earth and out into deep space, their mission failed.

Arrival at New Genesis

A blinding, nauseating surge of energy and light enveloped the flagship. Then, silence.

Dr. King gasped, clutching a handrail. The tactical screen had returned, no longer red, but filled with the green data of a pristine new environment. Through the bridge viewport, a sight of impossible beauty filled the vision: a sprawling, vibrant orange planet.

"Welcome home," Kofi whispered, a slow, genuine smile finally breaking his composure.

The atmosphere was crisp, the light brilliant, and the air clear of dust and smoke. Below them lay New Genesis, a world restored. The mission was complete. They had escaped the past, averted the final war, and preserved the future.

Kofi looked over the shoulder of the lieutenant who was monitoring the final Earth feed. Senator Thorne, alone in the dusty silo, was watching his own screen, which displayed the vanished fleet and the now-misguided nuclear missiles. A look of absolute defeat and terror crossed his face—not because he had failed to destroy the fleet, but because he was now permanently left behind with the ghost of his hatred.

Kofi turned away from the screen, his gaze fixed on the new world. "Anya, begin atmospheric scans. Dr. King, we have a civilization to build."

The Exodus was over. The Genesis had begun.

But that didn't happen.

Kofi chose another path for the fleet.

| 19 |

The Lunar Fracture

The peaceful, star-filled blackness of space was suddenly shattered by pure terror. On the bridge of The Promise, every screen was saturated with flashing red warnings.

"Temporal Shield—overload and deploy now!" Kofi roared, slamming his fingers onto the controls. He initiates the Magnetic Disruption Protocol. It works partially but is overwhelmed by the sheer nuclear force.

"Sixty seconds, Commander! It's too close!" shouted Jax, staring at rapidly approaching stealth missile trajectories.

A deafening KERR-CHUNK sound ripped through The Promise as the massive shield emitters unfolded, humming with a powerful, desperate blue light.

The Catastrophic Scar

"Impact in thirty seconds! Charging main shield!" Lieutenant Jax screamed.

Kofi stood at the command chair. "Initiate the Magnetic Disruption Protocol!"

The shield emitters unfolded from the ship's hull, humming with a powerful, desperate blue light. It worked initially: the outer ICBMs disintegrated harmlessly into inert atoms.

"It's holding!" Jemma yelled, with relief flooding her voice.

But then, the sheer power of the central warheads hit. There were too many, too close, and too volatile.

The massive, unstable blue energy from the defensive pulse merged with the raw force of the nuclear detonations. Instead of full disintegration, it created a concentrated, accidental beam of energy that lashed out.

The ship shuddered violently, thrown sideways by the feedback. The blue light faded, replaced by emergency red. The missiles were gone, but the silence was deafening.

Kofi scrambled back to the viewport. The Moon, usually their serene, silent guardian, looked wrong.

Anya pointed a trembling finger at the main viewport. "Commander, look at the Moon. The combined energy... it struck the surface."

Across the Moon's familiar, cratered surface was a sudden, hideous wound. A jagged, dark line of newly exposed rock—the Lunar Fracture—stretched hundreds of miles across its face. It was a massive, visible crack, glowing faintly with residual, catastrophic energy.

Kofi felt the cold horror of his fatal mistake. He had saved energy, but he had doomed the Earth. "My ancestors' first home," he whispered. "We were supposed to save them, not damage their future."

"Commander, Earth systems are already going offline!" Jax cried. "The gravity shift... the Fracture is destabilizing the planet! We have to leave now!"

Kofi grabbed the Temporal Sensor Key. "Jump," he commanded, his voice a low rumble of defeat. "One thousand years forward. And don't look back."

| 20 |

Catastrophe

The moment The Promise and the fleet vanished in that final, wrenching twist of reality, Earth was plunged into an eerie silence. The nuclear fires had faded, leaving behind an atmosphere heavy with dust and the silent, massive wound of the Lunar Fracture hanging in the night sky.

But the silence was quickly broken by the planet itself.

The Moon, now unbalanced by the catastrophic crack across its surface, had been pulled just slightly—a fraction of a degree—off its stable orbit. That small shift was enough to unleash a fury Earth had not seen since its primordial days. The final, devastating truth was clear to those who survived the initial hours: the planet was irreparably damaged.

Senator Thorne and his renegades had tried to destroy the future of the Travelers, but in doing so, they had condemned all of humanity to a slow, agonizing end.

The Super-Tides and Quaking Earth

The delicate, billions-of-years-old rhythm of the tides was violently shattered. What used to be a high tide became a colossal, churning wall of water.

Coastal cities were simply erased as tides rose hundreds of feet in minutes, not hours. Beaches were swallowed, and entire valleys became sudden inland seas, drawn by the Moon's new, erratic pull. Inland, rivers overflowed, and dams burst from the destabilized atmosphere's pressurized deluge.

As the water raged, the land began to revolt. The shift in the Moon's gravity and the pressure changes from the erratic tides were enough to shake the Earth's crust itself.

- Earthquakes: Fault lines that had been dormant for centuries ripped open. Massive earthquakes struck every continent simultaneously, causing skyscrapers to collapse and the ground to become liquid in places.
- Volcanic Activity: Volcanoes, long silent, belched massive clouds of ash and toxic gas into the sky, darkening the world further.
- Tsunamis: The forces were so great that continental plates ground against each other, causing tsunamis to cross entire ocean basins, meeting the super-tides and creating chaotic, impossible storms.

The Toxic Breath

The final death sentence for Earth was delivered from above. The force of the nuclear detonations, combined with the extreme geological upheaval, had effectively torn gaping holes in the atmosphere.

The ozone layer, the thin, invisible shield that protected all life, was gone in wide swaths. Deadly ultraviolet radiation poured through the new gaps, scorching everything it touched.

What wasn't ash and dust from the volcanoes and nuclear fallout was now filled with corrosive smog. Breathing became a painful, burning effort.

| 21 |

The Rescue Ark

The moment The Promise and the fleet vanished, Earth was plunged into an eerie silence, heavy with dust and the silent, massive wound of the Lunar Fracture hanging in the sky.

The Super-Tides and Toxic Breath

Earth was not going to vanish instantly, but it was irreparably damaged—shaking itself apart, drowning, and poisoning its inhabitants.

The Earth was dying. The ground had not stopped shaking for hours, and the air was a thick, burning soup of ash and poison.

On a high, crumbling rooftop in what used-to-be-Washington-DC, Senator Thorne and the last of his Global Purity Coalition agents watched the world end, coughing up black dust.

"They did this," Thorne snarled, pointing at the Lunar Fracture. "They destroyed us all."

The Ark's Return

It was then that the sky did the impossible. It ripped. A swirling vortex of dark blue and purple energy opened up over the suffering planet. And from that vortex, a shadow emerged.

It was not a ship. It was a world. The new vessel was so massive, it blocked out the fractured Moon entirely. The massive ship, The Ark, had jumped back to the moment after the disaster. The sky ripped open over the poisoned planet.

Kofi's voice boomed across the entire globe: "We are The Ark, and we are your only chance. We are taking everyone."

The Final Ransom

Massive, gentle columns of blue light descended from The Ark. They weren't the small, precise beams of the Exodus transports; these were enormous, city-wide transports, designed for one thing: mass evacuation.

The beams descended. They didn't check for race, or creed, or who was "good" or "bad." They simply lifted survivors. A blue light enveloped Senator Thorne and his men. He was being "rescued" by the very people he had tried to destroy. The beams raked across the dying planet, pulling up the last remnants of humanity, one desperate, terrified group at a time. The desperate escape of the Exodus had, through catastrophe, turned into a global Rescue Ark mission.

| 22 |

The Stowaways

Kofi surveyed the new population, recognizing the monumental problem they represented. He addressed his chief of security, a towering woman named Zara.

"Zara, isolate the Thorne group. They are a security risk but treat their wounds. Assign a team to the Stowaways. We need to know who they are, what they know, and what they can contribute. We need every single person."

In the Quarantine Bay, Dr. King began the interrogation of the key figures. The frustration was immense; even surrounded by the death of their world, Senator Thorne clung to entitlement, screaming about his rights as a US Senator. Thorne immediately turned aggressive, demanding to know why he was "kidnapped."

"You were found floating in the wreckage of a nuclear attack targeted at civilians," Dr. King retorted calmly. Thorne stammered, clinging to the old world's propaganda. "Kofi is a bioweapon, here to clean the slate and rebuild Earth for only one phenotype!"

The Revelation of Biological Necessity

The core stowaway group, including Lydia Shaw (Thorne's remorseful aide) and Thorne, were housed in a tightly monitored area. Dr. King then turned her attention to Lydia Shaw, Senator Thorne's former aide. The travelers resented feeding the people who had tried to drop nuclear bombs on them, but Dr. King defended Kofi's policy: "We are not defined by the hatred we fled, but by the mercy we offer."

Lydia confirmed the silo's location and Thorne's total control over the launch. But the tension escalated when Thorne doubled down on his entitlement and accused them of segregation: "You preach utopia, but you practice segregation!"

Dr. King finally revealed the truth: "We aren't segregating you, Thorne. We are bio-protecting you. The air where we are going would instantly destroy your lungs and skin. Your inability to survive our destination is a matter of physiology, not politics.

You are confined because we won't let you die." The massive fleet, now silent and stable, prepared for the most terrifying part of the journey: the journey through time itself.

This was the first time the stowaways understood the true, terrifying risk they posed to themselves. They were being kept alive not despite their biology, but because of it.

The fleet now carried the political and biological weight of Earth's past, and Kofi had to keep both sides stable. The massive, silent fleet, carrying the political and biological weight of 6 million lives, prepared for the 1000-year temporal jump.

| 23 |

The Temporal Revelation

The massive ship, The Ark, had jumped, but not into space. Dr. King stood on the silent, dimly lit bridge alongside Kofi, staring at the main viewport. The glass did not show stars streaming past; it showed something far more terrifying, time.

Kofi had activated the temporal drive—a technology so secret, only a handful of people even knew it existed. The air shimmered, smelling faintly of ozone and ancient metal. Outside the viewport, the Earth began to age in a terrifying time-lapse, moving at a rate of roughly one year per second.

The Catastrophic Future

The geological violence was breathtaking. The Earth's surface cracked like dry mud. They watched the fractured Moon's orbit decay in seconds, its massive pieces of rock raining down on the planet below. Oceans boiled, and the life-giving gases were scorched away.

Centuries flashed by in minutes. The beautiful blue marble turned into a churning, sickly brown. The atmosphere thinned, and the protective ozone layer burned away by solar radiation. The viewport showed the planet stabilize, yes, but in a state of utter toxicity. It was no longer Earth. It was a cinder.

Dr. King stood frozen, tears running down her face. "It's worse than we imagined. We failed."

The Truth of Aetheria

Kofi led Dr. King away from the viewport to a central holographic table. A 3D model of the damaged Earth shimmered above it.

"Dr. King," Kofi began, his eyes full of pain and determination. "There was no 'Great Ancestry' mission. The Travelers weren't chosen. They were the only ones who could survive the future. Our mission was a desperate, multi-century plan to travel back in time, collect a viable, healthy, and high-melanin population, and bring them forward to colonize the Earth's fragile recovery—the world we now call Aetheria.

He tapped the holographic globe, highlighting the toxic, high-UV light now bathing the planet.

Kofi explained that after the great fracture, the atmosphere collapsed, and the levels of Ultraviolet (UV) radiation became impossible.

"The people left behind the ones who didn't have the natural protection in their skin, began to die out slowly. Over centuries, they succumbed to the radiation." He looked directly at Dr. King. " Your ancestors—the people of the Travelers' fleet—survived because of one, necessary biological trait: melanin. The dark pigmentation in their skin was the only natural biological shield capable of allowing humans to endure the new environment."

Kofi's voice grew firm, ringing with finality.

The core scientific and philosophical revelation remains the same, regardless of the population size. The focus is on the why of the selection.

Kofi reveals: "The Travelers weren't chosen. They were the only ones who could survive the future... It was never about race. It was about survival physiology."

The truth hung heavy in the air. The final, desperate act was a ruthless, painful act of biological necessity. The exclusion of the others was not malice—it was a scientific mandate.

| 24 |

A Thousand Years Later

The world lurched. It wasn't the violent, heart-stopping lurch of the initial jump, but a soft, final deceleration. The time travel was over. One thousand years had passed for the universe outside, but only a few long minutes days for the six million people aboard The Ark.

Dr. King stood next to Kofi, gripping a rail as the massive viewport shimmered back into focus.

The Ark decelerated. What greeted them was Aetheria, the recovered Earth, glowing with a hazy, golden-orange hue.

The Welcoming Committee

Stepping onto the tarmac was a group of people unlike any the passengers had seen. These were the Aetherians—the descendants of the few Travelers left behind centuries ago to cultivate the future. They moved with an almost unnerving calm, dressed in clean, flowing materials that seemed to absorb the powerful light. They were all deeply melanated, possessing the biological shield necessary to thrive under Aetheria's golden sky.

Their leader, a woman named Soli (possessing the startling eyes of a thousand years of technological peace), approached the hatch.

"Welcome home, travelers," Soli said, her voice soft but strong. "We have waited for you. The mission was a success."

The Final Separation

The processing of the new arrivals began immediately. The Aetherians were high-tech, deeply organized, and profoundly peaceful. They didn't ask about race, politics, or wealth; they asked only: What skills do you bring?

While the successful Travelers were guided through orientation to Aetherian society—taught about the unique UV exposure hours, the diet, and the specific architecture—the Stowaways were immediately separated.

Soli explained the final plan to Dr. King: "They are our guests, but they are fragile. The UV levels in Aetheria's sunlight are immediately cytotoxic to their physiology. They cannot exist above ground."

Soli pointed to a large, specialized transport ship. "We have prepared a place for them. A sanctuary. A technological utopia of safety, engineered by our ancestors to provide every amenity of their former world, without the risk of the sun."

Kofi watched the final separation. "The future only needs people," he murmured to Dr. King. "And now, the final human family is here. The color of one's skin is no longer a mark of division, but the universal badge of a thousand years of survival." The final act of the Exodus was complete.

| 25 |

The New Utopia

The processing on Aetheria was swift, organized, and deeply insightful. The Aetherians, having prepared for this moment for a thousand years, quickly scanned every newcomer.

Within an hour, the separation began. Senator Thorne and Lydia Shaw, along with every other passenger who lacked the necessary deep melanin for high-UV resistance, were gently guided away. There were no arguments, just a quiet, immediate efficiency.

The Golden Cage: The Aegis Vault

The relocated group—now refugees—were led into a brilliant, futuristic elevator that dropped thousands of feet below the surface of Aetheria.

The doors opened onto a world of dazzling light and calm. This was The Aegis Vault, the underground sanctuary. It was a technological marvel: a sprawling, bio-filtered city sealed off entirely from the golden sunlight above. The ceilings were painted with dynamic images of old, pre-collapse Earth skies—blue, with soft, white clouds. Every need was met: clean water, customized education, entertainment, and endless, stable security. It was the perfect, safe utopia.

But the terrible catch was immediate. When Senator Thorne asked an attendant when they could see the real sky, the attendant gently replied, "This is your world, now. The surface of Aetheria... is too intense for your cellular structure. The ancient radiation lingers."

The thought hit Thorne with shocking clarity: They could never leave. They were saved, but they were permanently confined. Kofi hadn't just saved humanity; he had built two separate futures for it: one for the resilient above, and one for the sheltered below.

The Final Realization

Ten years after the Exodus, the new society was thriving. Dr. King, integrated into the surface council due to her engineering and past-world knowledge, often visited The Aegis Vault. She found Lydia Shaw teaching a new generation of stowaways about Earth's lost history, and Senator Thorne staring bitterly at the false ceiling, still convinced he was a prisoner.

One evening, Dr. King stood at an observation window overlooking the perpetual, controlled dusk of the underground city. She finally grasped the full, complicated tragedy and mercy of Kofi's command.

The Stowaways had fought to stay on an unstable, dying world, and now they had been given the very utopia they had denied others, but only as a necessary form of confinement.

Dr. King remembered Kofi's final, desperate words: "The mission is not to save everyone with the past's prejudices, but to save the last embers of human life, whatever the cost."

Dr. King stood at an observation window overlooking The Aegis Vault. Below her, the vast, subterranean city glowed brightly—a perfect utopia of perpetual, controlled dusk. She watched the millions of inhabitants living out their lives in total safety.

"The size of the task was immense," Dr. King murmured. "We built an entire second, invisible world just for their security."

Kofi looked at her. "The legacy of Aetheria is not just the technology we brought back, but the difficult ethical code we enforced. We chose life over politics. We chose survival over comfort."

Kofi offered the final hope: "The Aetherian scientists are working on genetic therapies and external shielding technology. One day, a thousand years from now, maybe The Aegis Vault's doors will open, and six million people will be able to join us under this sky."

The End.

ABOUT THE AUTHOR

Born and raised in The Bronx, New York—a proud product of John F. Kennedy High School—Tyrone Campbell brings a unique blend of street-smart grit and entrepreneurial vision to his fiction.

Tyrone is a true multi-hyphenate: a filmmaker, musician, and successful business owner. He first published his insights as a business coach in 2022, but now transitions to science fiction to explore the vast, complex societies he spent years building in his imagination.

This background allows him to write with rare authenticity, ensuring that the ambitious worlds he creates—like the technologically advanced, yet morally fragile future society of Aetheria in The Aetheria Covenant: The Exodus: A New Genesis—are grounded in logistical and economic realism.

When he's not crafting narrative, Tyrone is focused on creating his next venture or his next composition. He looks forward to writing and publishing more books that merge high-stakes drama with philosophical depth across multiple genres.